# Usborne Doodle Pad for Boys

## Illustrated by
## Maria Pearson and Lizzie Barber

Written by Kirsteen Robson

Designed by Karen Tomlins

# Fill the sky with fireworks.

Draw a surprising catch on the end of the line.

Doodle your own monster mug shots,
and give each one a name.

Doodle faces and feathers on the owls.

# Design some name labels.

Cover the leaves with hungry caterpillars.

Doodle someone crossing the tightrope,
then draw what might be underneath.

# Build an alien city.

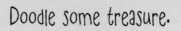

Doodle some treasure.

Doodle more feathers on the birds,
then give each one a juicy worm.

Doodle a crazy science experiment.

Add a picture, a name and a reward to this "Wanted" poster.

Doodle some friends for this dinosaur.

# Doodle spots and stripes on the beetles.

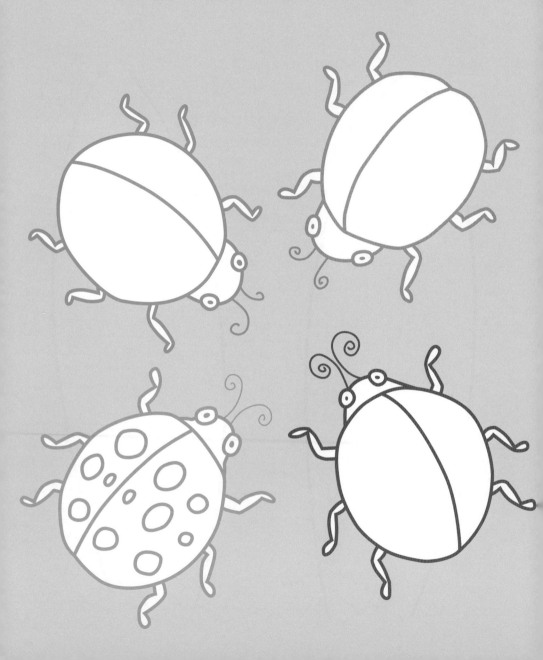

# Customize the surfboards.

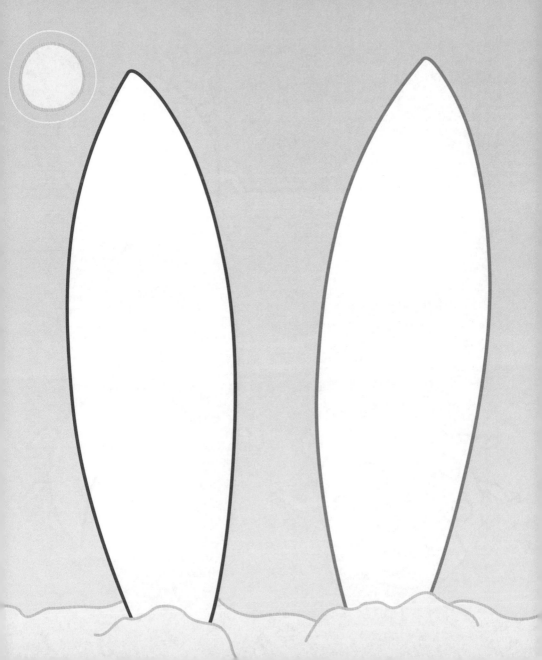

Fill the page with creepy crawlies.

Draw a monster that might live here.

# Draw more astronauts.

Add a message to put in the bottle.

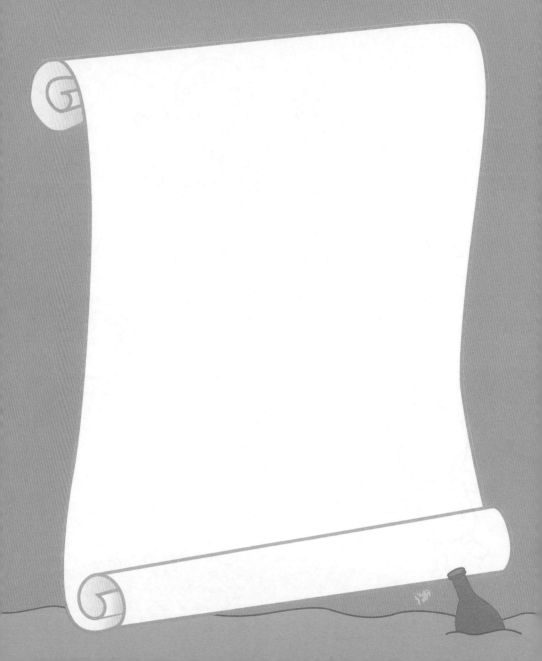

Give the sportsmen bats, balls and other sports equipment.

Doodle something this monster might find useful,
such as lots of socks and gloves, or some unusual sunglasses.

Draw what might be hovering over this city.

# Turn these squares into anything you like.

Doodle what you would take to a desert island.

# Draw some planes.

Doodle what might be on display in the window.

Customize the skateboards.

Design a control panel for the spaceship.

Draw one of these on each face and give each head some ears.

Give the alien more arms.

Doodle wheels, windows and people to
turn these rectangles into buses.

# Turn these shapes into beetles and other bugs.

# Add details to these boats.

# Doodle designs on the stamps.

# Give these monsters eyes and teeth.

Draw some penguins playing and swimming.

Give the crooked house more windows, walls, and a roof.

Doodle some disgusting toppings on this pizza.

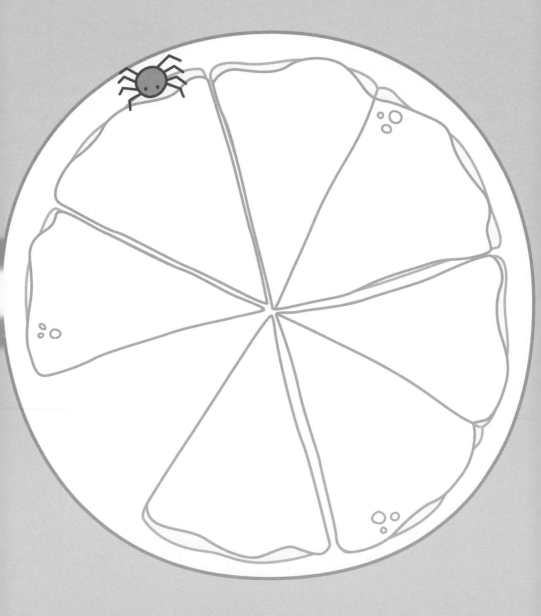

# Design a time machine.

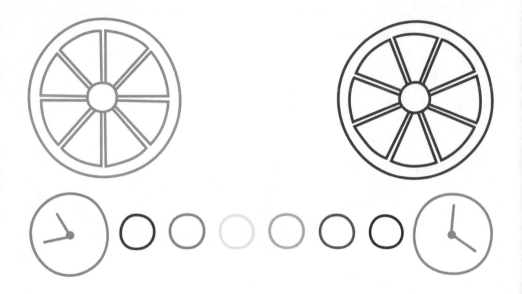

Design logos for teams you support.

Drip, drip, drop... doodle a shower of raindrops.

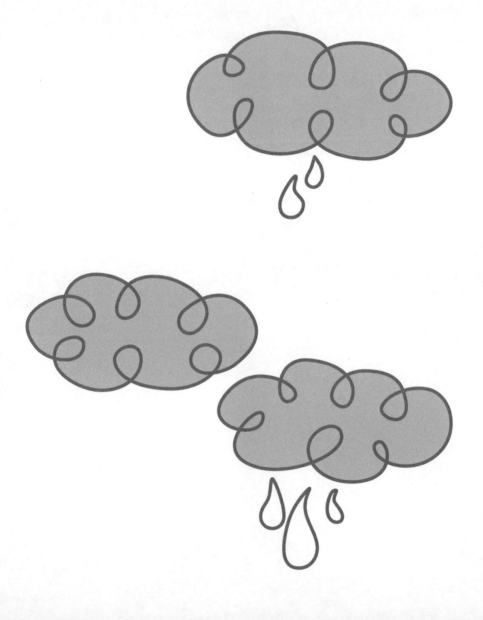

Add faces to the pumpkins.

Create a name plate for your door.

Doodle a tornado spinning across the page.

# Turn these circles into animals.

# Add some details to the treasure map.

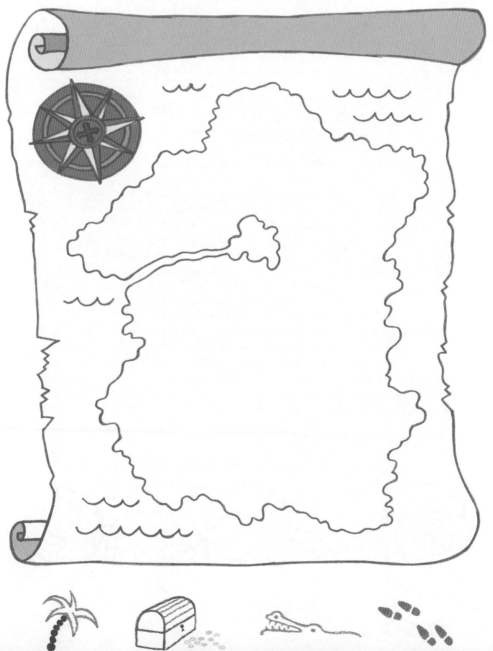

Design a door knocker.

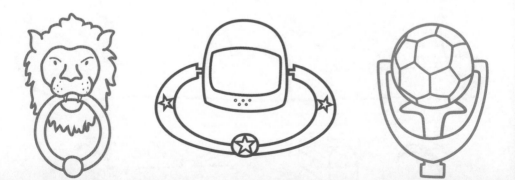

Turn these shapes into trucks, buses and cars.

# Draw more snowmen.

# Doodle some leaves falling from the tree.

Fill the page with circles.

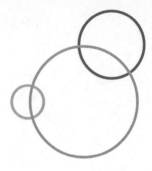

# Doodle on the sails.

Doodle a diver and then show who might be
watching him from the side of the pool.

# Design a bridge to cross the river.

Draw what might have escaped from these chains.

Give these flowers monster faces.

Add swirls of smoke to the chimneys.

# Fill the shapes to make 3-D effects.

Doodle some waves.

# Doodle designs on the warrior shields.

# Transform these shapes into robots.

# Design a castle.

Draw the other half of this owl.

Doodle some aliens in the spaceships.

Draw more birds on the branches.

Customize these cars.

Show what you might see under the magnifying glass.

Add more horrible things to the jar of goo.

Think of a title for this book then design a cover for it.

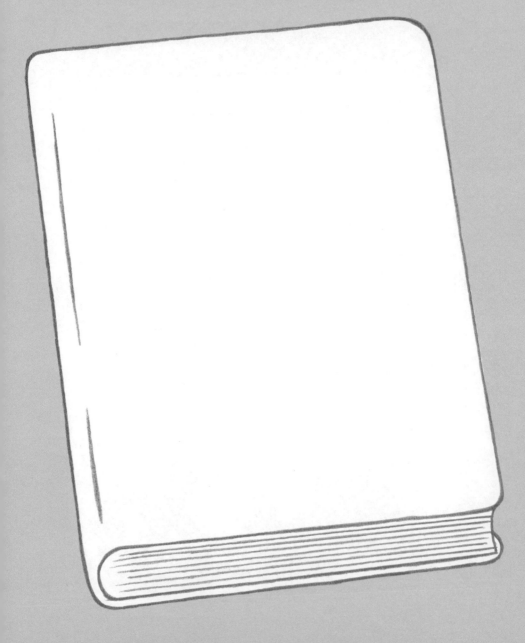

Doodle scales on the fish.

Draw the other half of Tutankhamun's mask.

# Draw more sharks.

Make this dragon breathe out flames, sparks or smoke.

# Transform these circles into anything you like.

Draw what you think might have been caught in the spotlight.

Doodle details on the robot.

# Design a lighthouse.

# Decorate the cookies.

# Turn these shapes into snack bar wrappers.

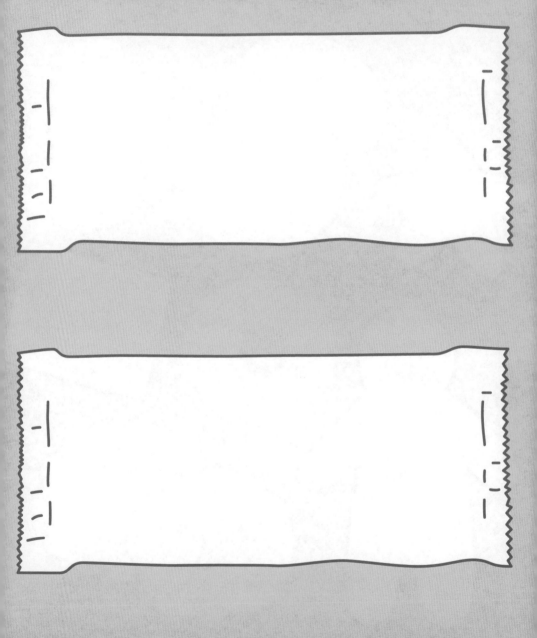

# Add windows and markings to these planes.

Turn this shape into a monster.

Draw what this giant magnet might have attracted.

Create a superhero. What special powers does he have?

# Draw something appearing out of the magician's hat.

# Doodle some friends for this monster.

# Doodle more skydivers and give them parachutes.

Doodle markings on the big cats.

Make the volcano erupt.

Design a novelty hot-air balloon.

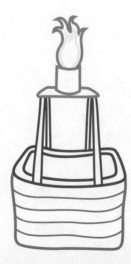

# Transform these shapes into insects.

# Use all kinds of creature features to make up an animal, then give it a name.

Hippopotamouse

Skalligator

Zebraphant

# Draw the rest of the castle.

# Arrange some presents under the tree.

Turn these circles into spiders.

# Doodle faces and hair.

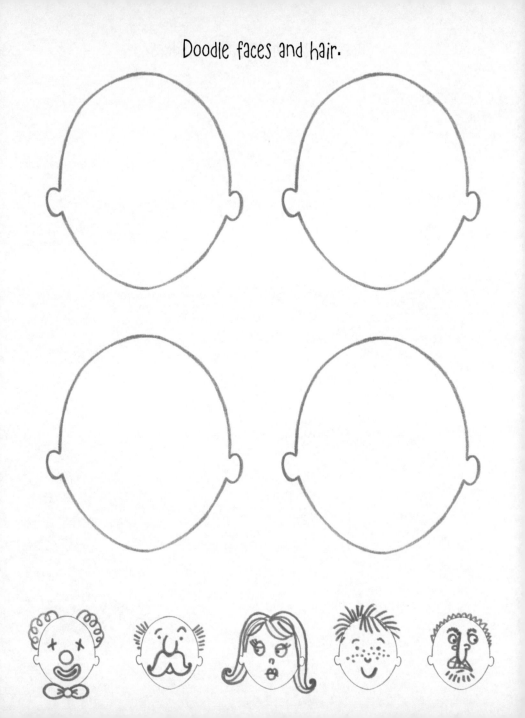

Design a new look for your team.

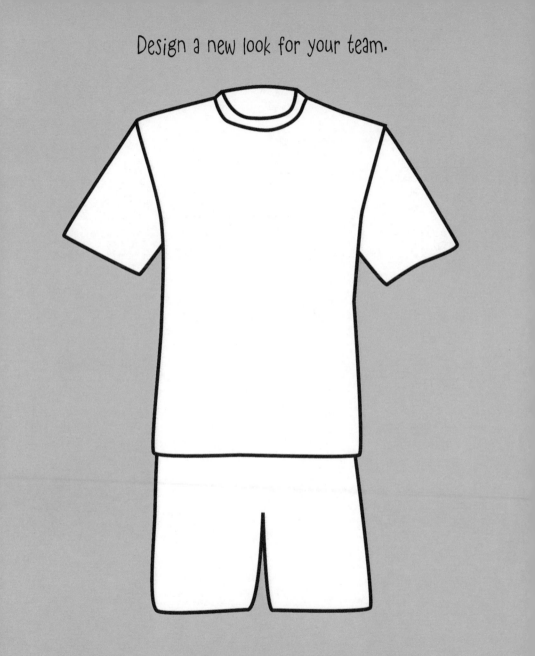

Doodle more footprints and tracks in the snow.

Add birds or eggs to the nest.

Design a monster truck.

Doodle markings on the lizards.

Draw what the seedling might grow into.

Doodle sharp spikes on the cactus plants.

# Draw monsters around these eyes.

Draw more bats.

# Make these shapes look like penguins.

# Give these monsters faces.

# Design yourself a coat of arms.

Fill the jars.

# Transform these shapes into cats.

# Turn these shapes into aliens.

Draw a rocket blasting off.

# Draw some dogs in the park.

# Add more cars to the collection.

Add some waves and birds.

Draw the other half of this spaceship.

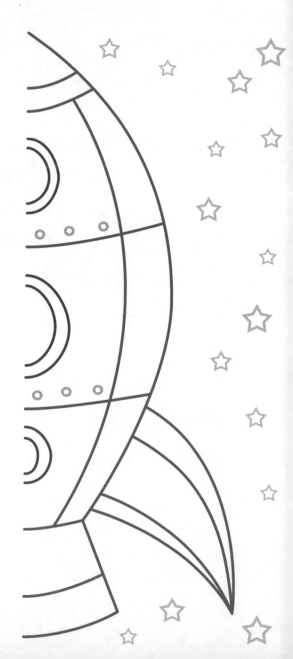

Finish the sails by adding race numbers and team logos.

Give this sea monster more tentacles,
then show what you think it has caught with them.

# Design an underwater vehicle.

Finish drawing this astronaut.

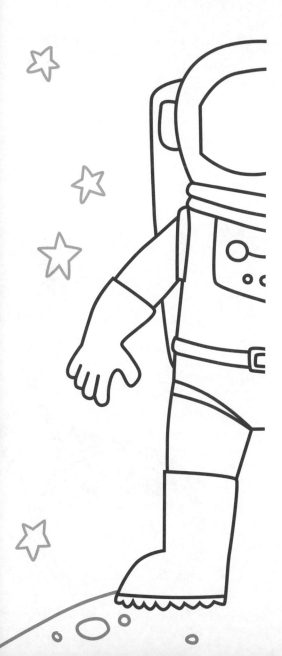

# Make these shapes into bees.

Doodle a maze between the mouse and the cheese.

# Design a submarine.

Show what is hatching out of the egg.

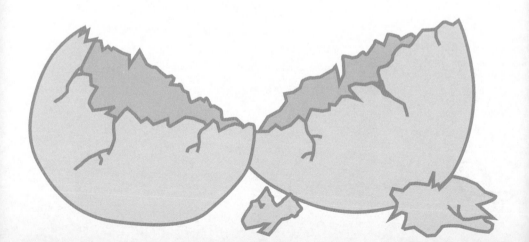

# Turn these shapes into faces.

# Finish the web and add a spider.

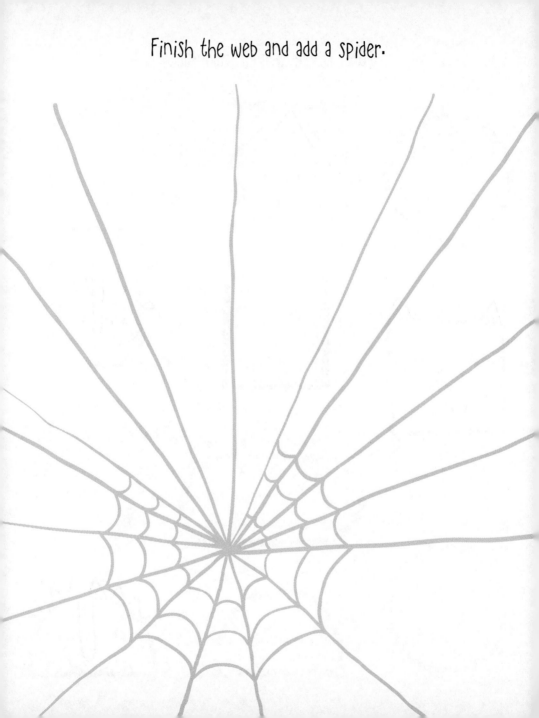

# Turn this shape into a house or castle.

Design a starship.

# Draw a picture of your ideal destination, then add a message.

Dear

We are staying...

The weather is...

We have been to...

From

Complete this dinosaur.

Draw what might be beyond the gates.

# Turn these shapes into flying machines.

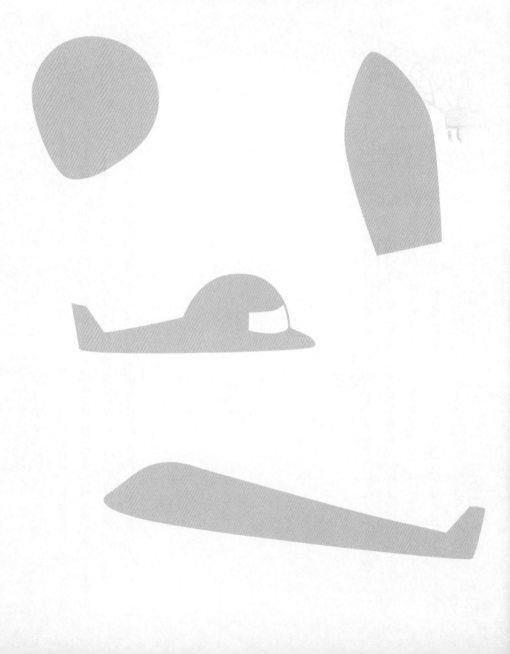

# Fill the coral reef with fish and bubbles.

Draw what might be standing on the plinths and pillars.

Doodle some supersize waves around this surfer.

Draw who or what might be standing in the spotlight.

# Doodle aliens in the craters.

# Turn these shapes into animals.

Draw another knight next to this one.

Doodle some noodles.

# Customize these sports helmets.

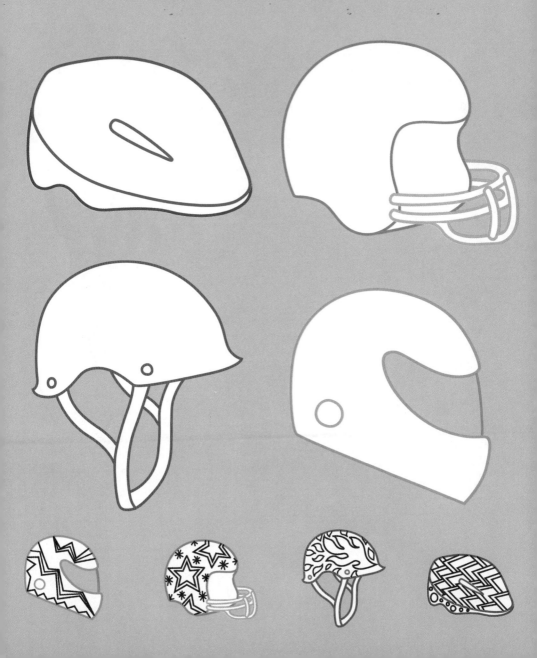

# Doodle some patterns the skaters have made.

# Doodle ski tracks in the mountain snow.

Use straight lines to continue the doodle.

Doodle patterns on the hot-air balloons.

# Draw more spaceships.

# Doodle patterns on the snakes.

# Give these gargoyles ugly faces.

Draw a prize-winning hedge sculpture.

Doodle what a monster might have in its kitchen.

Draw what the pirate is dreaming about.

# Add some dolphins.

Add more ants to the march.

Doodle kites on the strings.

Doodle on the ship, then add some fish and sharks.

# Add alien faces to these shapes.

Draw a friend for this robot.

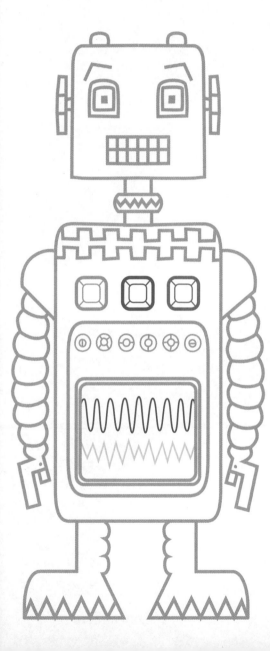

Give these dinosaurs horns, spikes, frills or crests.

# Fill the page with dangerous fish.

# Doodle something for each animal to eat.

# Draw triangles inside triangles, inside triangles...

# Doodle a dancing skeleton.

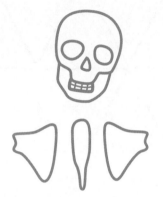

Show what's happening beneath the city.

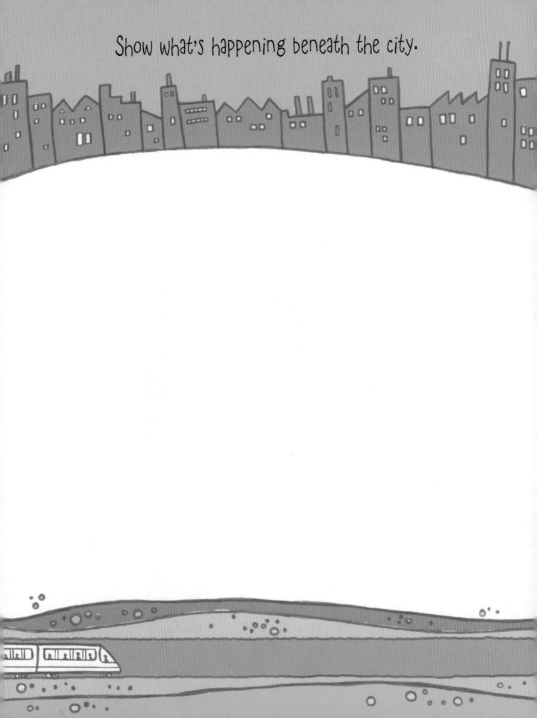

Fill the page with stars.

# Doodle some funny faces.

# Doodle sea creatures around these eyes.

# Finish drawing the sea monster.

Add some buildings then doodle lots of windows.

Doodle pebbles and starfish on the beach.

# Add rain, snow and lightning to the clouds.

Draw the dream.

Give the chicks eyes, beaks and legs.

Draw what is chasing these little dinosaurs.

Doodle some hair.

Doodle designs on the shields, flags and banners.

# Design some flags.

# Add to this design for an amazing invention. What can it do?

Draw something that might own these teeth.

Draw peas in the pods.

# Add more rabbits to the scene.

Design a robot.

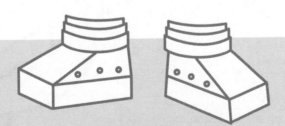

Turn the shapes into birds, or anything else you like.

Doodle eyes, noses and mouths.

# Transform these clouds into animals.

Give these caterpillars boots.

Add more towers and turrets to the sandcastle.

Fill the swamp with crocodiles.

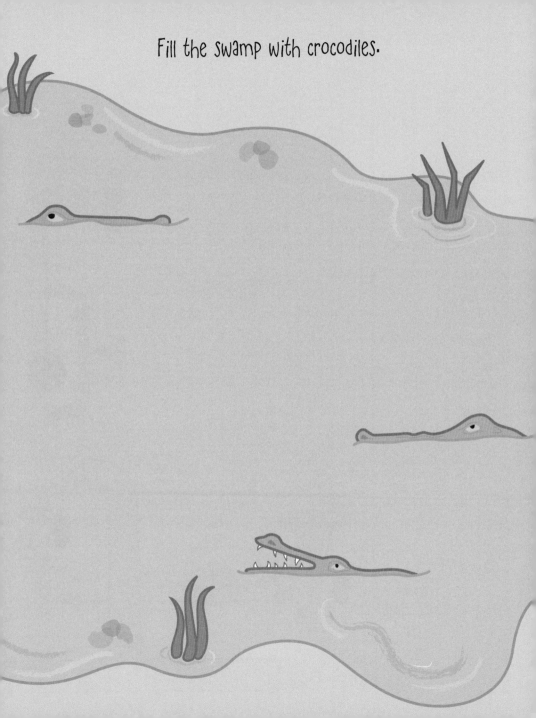

Doodle more pipes.

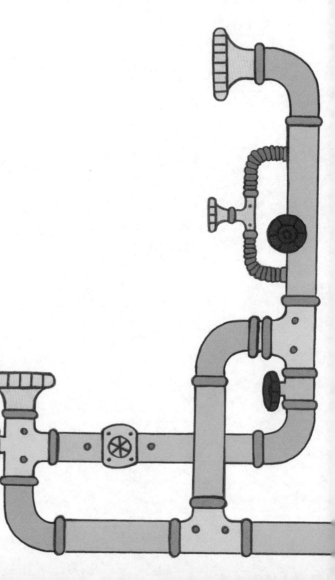

# Take this line for a walk without crossing over a line you have already drawn.

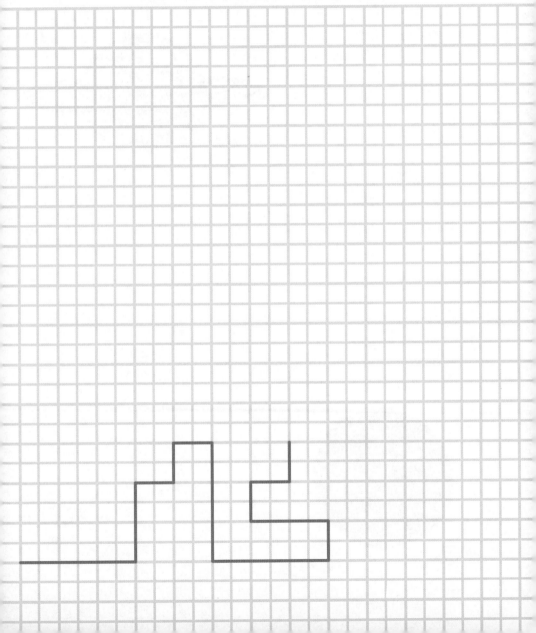

# Doodle some more stars and planets.

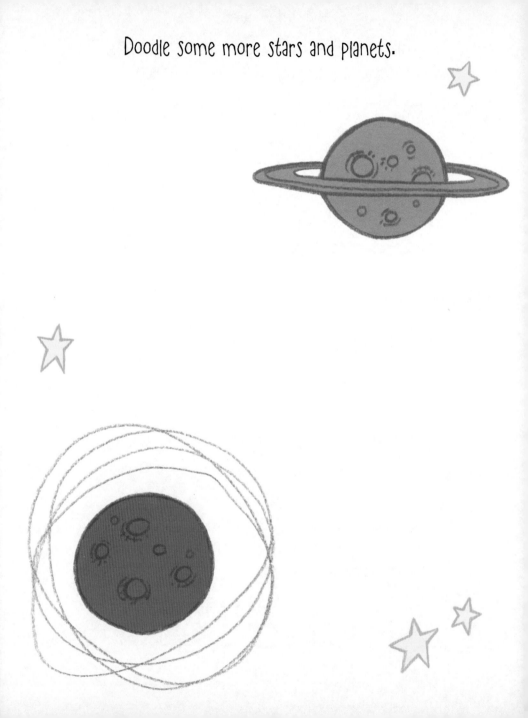

Draw something that these feet might belong to.

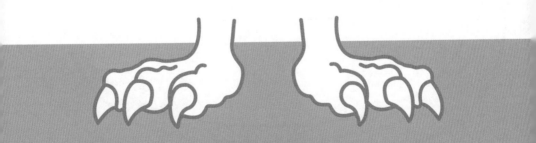

Draw what might have frightened this swimmer.

# Customize the T-shirts.

# Doodle some bubbles.

Draw the person who owns these boots.

# Add more buildings to the lost underwater city.

Draw a pond, then doodle some ripples, fish and reeds.

Add details to the medals to show what
each one might be awarded for.

Draw the other half of this monster.

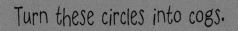

Turn these circles into cogs.

Give these monster plants teeth, spikes or thorns.

Turn these slugs into snails by designing homes for them.

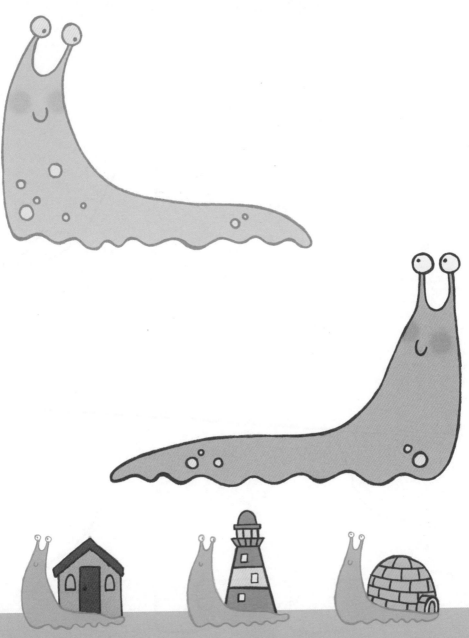

# Copy the details on the top dinosaur onto the bottom one.

Draw this monster's friends and relations.

# Turn these shapes into pirate faces.